SNOW DOG

MALORIE BLACKMAN

Illustrated by Sami Sweeten

www.randomhousechildrens.co.uk

D0267413

For Neil and Lizzy, with love,
and for Donnika — as promised!

SNOW DOG
A CORGI BOOK 978 0 552 56891 3

Published in Great Britain by Corgi Books,
an imprint of Random House Children's Publishers UK
A Random House Group Company

Corgi Pups edition published 1998
This Colour First Reader edition published 2013

1 3 5 7 9 10 8 6 4 2

J308.955
£7.50

Set in Bembo MT Schoolbook 21pt/28pt

Corgi Books are published by Random House Children's Publishers UK,
61–63 Uxbridge Road, London W5 5SA

www.**randomhousechildrens**.co.uk
www.**randomhouse**.co.uk

Addresses for companies within The Random House Group Limited can be found at:
www.randomhouse.co.uk/offices.htm

THE RANDOM HOUSE GROUP Limited Reg. No. 954009

A CIP catalogue record for this book is available from the British Library.

Printed in Italy.

Contents

COLOUR FIRST READER books are perfect for
beginner readers. All the text inside this Colour First
Reader book has been checked and approved by a
reading specialist, so it is the ideal size, length
and level for children learning to read.

Series Reading Consultant: Prue Goodwin
Honorary Fellow of the University of Reading

Chapter One
Grandad's Idea

Nicky lived with her mum and her dad in a beautiful house with lots of rooms. The house had a big garden at the front and an even bigger garden at the back. But Nicky was miserable.

She didn't mind not having
any brothers or sisters, but there
was one thing she wanted more
than anything else in the world.

"Mum, *please* can I have a
dog?"

"You must be joking, sweet pea," sniffed Nicky's mum as she hunted for her handbag.

"Why not?"

"Because a dog would make a mess of our carpets," said Nicky's mum, as she searched in her handbag for her front door keys.

"We could make a kennel for it in our back garden," Nicky tried.

"In the garden?" Nicky's mum was horrified. "Where it could dig up my tulips and my pansies and my roses? Are you crazy? I don't think so, poppet."

And Mum rushed off to work.

"Dad, can I have a dog *please*?" Nicky pleaded, as Dad came downstairs.

"I'm afraid not, precious."

"But why not?" Nicky was trying not to cry.

"Because, my apple dumpling, your mum and I work during the day and you're at school, so who would look after it?" said Dad.

"I would when I got home from school," Nicky replied eagerly. "No, honey muffin. Dogs need to be exercised regularly – through rain or shine, snow or hail. You're too young to take a dog for regular walks and your mum and I are too busy. It just wouldn't work." Dad rummaged through the notes and letters on the hall table looking for the shopping list. "Ah, there it is!"

Dad tucked the list into his shirt pocket.

"Couldn't we try, just for a while?" Nicky pleaded.

"No, angel lips. I'm sorry, but no." And Dad headed out of the door to do the shopping.

 Tears started to stream down Nicky's face. Grandad, who had been watching everything from the living room, came out into the hall holding the biggest hankie she had ever seen. Grandad's hankie was almost the size of a tablecloth!

"Never mind, Nicky. Use my hankie to dry your eyes. Don't worry, it's clean!" And Grandad dropped the whole thing down on Nicky's head. It covered her face like a huge and very floppy hat.

"Grandad!" Nicky laughed as she pulled it off. "I haven't got twenty eyes spread out all over my head!"

"That's my girl," Grandad grinned. "Cheer up, treasure."

"Oh Grandad, I wish you lived closer so that we could see you more often. Then maybe Mum and Dad would let me have a dog – if you could be here to look after it," Nicky sighed.

"Don't worry, sweetie. Dry your eyes and I'll tell you about my idea."

"What idea?" asked Nicky, wiping her eyes.

"Do you really
and truly want a
dog?" asked Grandad.

"Mum and Dad won't let me
have one." Nicky sniffed, her eyes
itching with fresh tears.

"They won't buy one for you,
but I know how we could get
you a dog of your very own."
Grandad's eyes were twinkling.

"How?"

"We could make
one!" said
Grandad.

Chapter Two
Waiting

"Make one?" Nicky stared at her grandad.

"That's right."

"How on earth can we make our own dog?" asked Nicky.

"Come with me." Grandad
led the way into the living room.
"Now then, where did I put it?"

"Put what?"

"My bag," said Grandad
looking around.

"It's over there, next to the telly." Nicky wondered how Grandad could miss it! His bag was gigantic and Mum and Dad were always complaining that it looked like Grandad was carrying a huge scatter cushion on his shoulder. J308.955

"Right then, stand back!"
Grandad bent down and buried
his head in the bag. It looked like
he was diving right into it. Nicky
watched as Grandad started
throwing out all kinds of things,

22

like a yellow lampshade and an
electric kettle and a half-eaten
packet of chocolate biscuits.
Several books, a few CDs and a
computer keyboard flew across
the room after the biscuits.

"Ah! Here it is!" exclaimed Grandad at last. "The very thing."

"What is it?" Nicky couldn't resist going closer to see.

"It's a snow dome kit. It's got a dome and the base and glitter and bits of plastic we can use for snow and it's got extra-special clay that we can use to make your dog."

"What's extra-special about it?" asked Nicky.

"I found this clay at the end of the most beautiful rainbow I've ever seen in my life," said Grandad. "I dug it up myself. And everyone knows rainbows are made of wishes and are very special. So any dog made with this clay will be extra-special. Maybe even magic . . ."

"A clay dog isn't the same as having a real dog." Nicky sighed.

"We'll see," winked Grandad. "We'll see."

For the next hour, Grandad and Nicky sat at the table making a snow dome dog.

Nicky made
the body and
the face and
Grandad made
the tail and the legs.
Nicky gave her dog big, floppy
ears and, very carefully, she
turned up the corners of the
puppy's mouth. And she turned
his tail up too, to show that he
was wagging it.

"That's better. He looks like a happy dog now." Nicky sat back, satisfied.

At last it was finished.

"Now we have to bake it until it's quite hard," said Grandad. "And then we can paint it."

When at last the dog had baked and was cool enough to paint, Nicky did that all by herself. She painted her dog a golden brown with dark brown eyes and silver paws.

"Perfect!" said Grandad. "Now we just have to wait for the paint to dry."

 As soon as
the paint was
dry, Nicky
very carefully
attached the
puppy to the base of the dome.
Grandad filled the glass dome
with water and asked, "Shall we
put in the snow or some glitter?"

"The snow," Nicky replied at once.

"Snow it is then," said Grandad. And he tipped the packet of white plastic snow into the water in the dome.

Grandad turned the base upside down and screwed it onto the dome, before clicking it into place.

He turned the dome the right way round and handed it over to his granddaughter. "And here it is! Your very own snow dog!"

"I'm going to call him Harry," Nicky decided with a smile. "Hello, Harry. Aren't you pretty?" She gave her snow dome a shake. The plastic snow fell all around Harry and looked just like real snow.

"Can I take him into the garden?" Nicky asked.

"Of course. Take a jumper though. It's a bit chilly out there."

"Chilly! It's baking out there!" Nicky glanced out of the window. There wasn't a cloud in the summer sky and the sun was blazing down.

"Jumper, please!" Grandad insisted.

Nicky ran upstairs to get a jumper. She tied it around her waist rather than put it on.

Grandad might be cold, but she certainly wasn't. She ran back downstairs to the kitchen.

"Out you go then," nodded Grandad when he saw Nicky had her jumper. "I'll call you when it's lunch-time."

So off Nicky went. She sat on her swing, twisting her legs this way, then that. She shook the snow dome again.

Harry was indeed the most beautiful dog in the world. Nicky sighed, a deep, unhappy sigh.

"I wish you were real, then I could play in there with you," she whispered.

A very strange thing began to happen. The snow dome grew colder and colder as Nicky held it, until it felt like she was holding a snowball at the North Pole! But that was impossible. It was the middle of summer and the sun was shining like a brand new coin.

Nicky put the snow dome down on the grass and blew on her fingers. They were almost numb. She frowned down at the dome. What was going on?

"Oh my goodness!" Nicky exclaimed.

Harry was wagging his tail. He was actually wagging his tail! And now he was barking. A very tiny, faint sound but it was definitely a bark.

Chapter Three
Harry

Nicky blinked once, blinked twice and then it happened. The third time she blinked, she opened her eyes to find herself standing in front of a real, live, furry Harry. And there was snow falling all around them.

"How woof-onderful!" said Harry. "You've come to play with me. I hoped you would!"

"You can talk too?" Nicky asked, amazed.

"Of course," Harry said. "All dogs talk! At least, they do in here. Isn't it woof-onderful?"

Nicky couldn't believe it. She was *inside* the dome and just a bit bigger than Harry. Grandad had said the clay might be magic. Nicky looked around. What a beautiful place! Somewhere, far off in the distance, lights

twinkled just like fairy lights on a
Christmas tree.

And here and there were fir
and pine trees, swaying to and
fro in the wind as if they were
waving at Nicky to welcome her.
And the air smelt crisp and clean.

Nicky took a delighted deep breath. There was just one thing wrong.

"Brrrr! It's freezing in here!"
"Put on your jumper then,"
Harry suggested.

Nicky had completely forgotten about the jumper tied around her waist. She untied it and quickly pulled it on. Much, much better! She wasn't the least bit cold now. Funny it should be so cold when the snow was only plastic. Nicky put out her hand.

Snow fell on it, melting away just like real snowflakes.

From the outside, the dome looked like plastic and clay and glass, but on the inside everything was real. What a weird, wonderful place!

"So what're we going to play first?"

"Play?"

"Well, that is why you made me isn't it? So we can play together?" said Harry.

Nicky nodded. She wasn't sure how to play with a snow dog but she was certainly willing to learn.

"Throw a snowball and I'll fetch it!" said Harry.

"But it'll melt in your mouth," Nicky laughed.

"Try it," Harry insisted.

So Nicky picked up a handful
of snow and squeezed it together
until it was ball-shaped, then she
threw it as hard as she could.

In a flash, Harry was off chasing after it. And to Nicky's surprise, he came trotting back to her with the snowball still intact in his mouth.

"This is a funny, fantastic place," Nicky laughed.

"Woof-onderful!" Harry agreed.

Nicky and Harry spent the afternoon playing together. First they played fetch with snowballs, then they chased each other and Nicky didn't get cold once. She didn't even get the slightest bit chilly, even though the snow

kept falling and she was only
wearing a jumper and shorts and
her trainers. And it didn't matter
how far or how fast they ran,
they never ran into the sides of
the dome. In fact, Nicky couldn't
even see the sides of the dome.

I must be very, very small,
Nicky thought to herself. Funny,
but I don't feel small. In fact,
just the opposite. Now she had a
friend, she felt like a giant!

After that, they made angels
in the snow. Nicky lay on her
back and moved her arms up

and down at her sides so she
could make the pattern of
wings and Harry lay on his
front and moved his front paws
up and down. Nicky couldn't
remember when she'd had so
much fun. Having a dog was
just as she'd imagined it.

"Nicky, you'd better think about getting back. Your grandad will be wondering where you are," Harry pointed out.

Nicky couldn't bear it. "Oh, Harry! I can come back and play with you again, can't I?"

 "Of course you can." Harry wagged his tail. "And I'll be right here waiting for you."

Nicky picked up Harry and cuddled him. "Oh, it's not fair. I wish you could come out of this dome and be with me."

Oh dear! The snow began to whirl around them faster and faster and it

began to snow *upwards* instead of downwards.

"What's going on?" Nicky called out.

And before she could say another word, she was back in her garden with the snow dome on the grass at her feet and the sun blazing down on her back. And Harry had grown to the size of a real dog and he was standing right in front of her, his golden brown fur and silver paws gleaming in the sun.

"The wish came true." Nicky clapped her hands. "It must be something to do with the rainbow clay. It's made all my wishes come true. Now you can be with me always and for ever and we'll never . . ."

"Nicky, I don't feel well . . ." Harry began, before his voice trailed off altogether. Something was wrong. Harry was in trouble.

 "It's too hot. It hurts . . ." Harry cried out.

And horrified, Nicky watched as Harry's golden fur began to bubble like overheated porridge. And the silver fur of his paws began to chip and flake, fluttering like moonlit rain onto the grass below.

Chapter Four
The Final Wish

"No! Harry, No!" Nicky knelt down in front of Harry to try and protect him from the sun's rays but it was no good. A tiny crack, no thicker than a hair, appeared on one of his ears.  He was starting to crumble. "I can't stay here.

It's too hot for me," Harry gasped.

"Quick! You've got to go back

into the snow dome,"
Nicky said urgently.

"How?" asked
Harry. "I don't know
how I came *out* of the dome, so

I certainly don't
know how to
get back in."

Nicky thought
desperately.

"I wished it," Nicky realized.
"I wished you would leave the
dome and be with me for
always."

"If you don't *un*wish it and soon, there'll be nothing left of me but dust!" Harry said, lying down. The gold of his fur was flaking faster now. Nicky had to do something. She *had* to. She picked up the dome and held it tightly in both hands.

"Harry, I want you to stay with me so much but not if it's going to make you ill or fall to

pieces, so I wish you were back
in the dome where you'll be cold
and safe and happy."

Before Nicky could blink
Harry had disappeared.

"Harry? Harry, are you in
there? Are you OK?" Nicky held
the snow dome up to her face
and shook it frantically. "Harry?"

"Ah! That's much better," Harry barked happily. He ran around in circles chasing his wagging tail.

"Oh Harry, thank goodness. I'm so glad you're safe." Nicky grinned with relief.

"Nicky, come in for your lunch," called Grandad from the kitchen door.

Nicky leapt to her feet, still holding the snow dome in her hands. "Grandad, did you see . . . ?"

"Shush! I don't want anyone to know that I'm real, except you," said Harry.

"Did I see what?" Grandad prompted.

"Nothing!" Nicky shook her head, hiding her snow dome behind her back.

"Come in now, dear," said Grandad.

"I'll be right there." Nicky waited until Grandad disappeared back into the house before she turned to Harry. "Harry, I've just thought of something," she said.

"If I'm out here and you're in there, how will we play together again? Will I be able to get back into the dome and be with you?"

"If you hold onto the dome
with both hands and really, really
wish for it to happen, then it will,"
said Harry.

"D'you think
so?" said Nicky
anxiously. "You
don't think all your
rainbow clay magic is used up
yet?"

 "Nicky, I'm
not the only
one who's
magic," Harry
laughed. "Didn't you know
that you are too?"

"Me?" asked Nicky, amazed.

"You!" said Harry.

And then Nicky understood. "So it's not the rainbow clay that's magic, is it? It's you and me — together."

"Exactly." And Harry started chasing his tail again.

Nicky laughed. "Harry, you and I are going to have such fun together."

"Of course we are!" said Harry.

"It's going to be woof-onderful!" said Nicky and Harry together.

And laughing, Nicky carried Harry back into her house. It was time for lunch!

THE END

Colour First Readers

Welcome to Colour First Readers. The following pages are intended for any adults (parents, relatives, teachers) who may buy these books to share the stories with youngsters. The pages explain a little about the different stages of learning to read and offer some suggestions about how best to support children at a very important point in their reading development.

Children start to learn about reading as soon as someone reads a book aloud to them when they are babies. Book-loving babies grow into toddlers who enjoy sitting on a lap listening to a story, looking at pictures or joining in with familiar words. Young children who have listened to stories start school with an expectation of enjoyment from books and this positive outlook helps as they are taught to read in the more formal context of school.

Cracking the code

Before they can enjoy reading for and to themselves, all children have to learn how to crack the alphabetic code and make meaning out of the lines and squiggles we call letters and punctuation. Some lucky pupils find the process of learning to read undemanding; some find it very hard.

Most children, within two or three years, become confident at working out what is written on the page. During this time they will probably read collections of books which are graded; that is, the books introduce a few new words and increase in length, thus helping youngsters gradually to build up their growing ability to work out the words and understand basic meanings.

Eventually, children will reach a crucial point when, without any extra help, they can decode words in an entire book, albeit a short one. They then enter the next phase of becoming a reader.

Making meaning

It is essential, at this point, that children stop seeing progress as gradually 'climbing a ladder' of books of ever-increasing difficulty. There is a transition stage between building word recognition skills and enjoying reading a story. Up until now, success has depended on getting the words right but to get pleasure from reading to themselves, children need to fully comprehend the content of what they read. Comprehension will only be reached if focus is put on understanding meaning and that can only happen if the reader is not hesitant when decoding. At this fragile, transition stage, decoding should be so easy that it slowly becomes automatic. Reading a book with ease enables children to get lost in the story, to enjoy the unfolding narrative at the same time as perfecting their newly learned word recognition skills.

At this stage in their reading development, children need to:

- Practice their newly established early decoding skills at a level which eventually enables them to do it automatically

- Concentrate on making sensible meanings from the words they decode

- Develop their ability to understand when meanings are 'between the lines' and other use of literary language

- Be introduced, very gradually, to longer books in order to build up stamina as readers

In other words, new readers need books that are well within their reading ability and that offer easy encounters with humour, inference, plot-twists etc. In the past, there have been very few children's books that provided children with these vital experiences at an early stage. Indeed, some children had to leap from highly controlled teaching materials to junior novels.

This experience often led to reluctance in youngsters who were not yet confident enough to tackle longer books.

Matching the books to reading development

Colour First Readers fill the gap between early reading and children's literature and, in doing so, support inexperienced readers at a vital time in their reading development. Reading aloud to children continues to be very important even after children have learned to read and, as they are well written by popular children's authors, Colour First Readers are great to read aloud. The stories provide plenty of opportunities for adults to demonstrate different voices or expression and, in a short time, give lots to talk about and enjoy together.

Each book in the series combines a number of highly beneficial features, including:

• Well-written and enjoyable stories by popular children's authors

• Unthreatening amounts of print on a page

• Unrestricted but accessible vocabularies

- A wide interest age to suit the different ages at which children might reach the transition stage of reading development

- Different sorts of stories – traditional, set in the past, present or future, real life and fantasy, comic and serious, adventures, mysteries etc.

- A range of engaging illustrations by different illustrators

- Stories which are as good to read aloud to children as they are to be read alone

All in all, Colour First Readers are to be welcomed for children throughout the early primary school years – not only for learning to read but also as a series of good stories to be shared by everyone. I like to think that the word 'Readers' in the title of this series refers to the many young children who will enjoy these books on their journey to becoming lifelong bookworms.

Prue Goodwin
Honorary Fellow of the University of Reading

Helping children to enjoy *Snow Dog*

If a child can read a page or two fluently, without struggling with the words at all, then he/she should be able to read this book alone. However, children are all different and need different levels of support to help them become confident enough to read a book to themselves.

Some young readers will not need any help to get going; they can just get on with enjoying the story. Others may lack confidence and need help getting into the story. For these children, it may help if you talk about what might happen in the book.

Explore the title, cover and first few illustrations with them, making comments and suggestions about any clues to what might happen in the story. Read the first chapter aloud together. Don't make it a chore. If they are still reluctant to do it alone, read the whole book with them, making it an enjoyable experience.

The following suggestions will not be necessary every time a book is read but, every so often, when a story has been particularly enjoyed, children love responding to it through creative activities.

Before reading

You may need to explain what a snow dome is before starting this book. The story, *Snow Dog*, could be described as magical fantasy. What happens could be in the imagination of a little girl who desperately wants a dog or it could all be about 'a dream come true'.

For young children, it is natural that they 'believe' some things that are actually imaginary (tooth fairies and Santa Claus, for example); Grandads who can do magic come into that category. So let imagination take over as you share this book.

During reading

Asking questions about a story can be really helpful to support understanding but don't ask too many – and don't make it feel like test on what has happened. Relate the questions to the child's own experiences and imagination. For example, ask: 'Why do you think Nicky wants a dog so much?' and 'I wonder if Grandad can do magic. What do you think?' Perhaps there is a person in your family who is a bit like Grandad.

Responding to the book

If your child has enjoyed the story, it increases the fun by doing something creative in response. If possible, provide art materials and dressing up clothes so that they can make things, play at being characters, write and draw, act out a scene or respond in some other way to the story.

Activities for children

If you have enjoyed reading this story, you could:

• Make a tiny dog with modelling clay.

• Count how many 'pet names' (e.g. 'darling', 'sweetheart') are given to Nicky in Chapter 1. Pet names show how much someone loves you. Do members of your family call you by pet names? Here are some of the names with letters missing. Can you find them in the book and fill in the missing letters?

1. sw___ p___   2. po____

3. pr_____   4. my ap___ d_____

5. hon__ m_____   6. angel ____

7. tr_____   8. sw_____

• Write a list of the things Grandad had in his big bag. Can you find any clues that show us that Grandad might be able to do magic.

- Draw and label a comic strip of four pictures (one for each page) to show what happened from page 34 to page 37. You can use the illustrations to help you or do your own original pictures. You can add speech or thought bubbles to the drawings.

- Make up a new adventure for Nicky and Harry.

ALSO AVAILABLE AS COLOUR FIRST READERS